HANSEL, GRETEL, and the PUDDING PLOT

BY ISABEL THOMAS

ILLUSTRATED BY MÓNICA CARRETERO

picture
window
books
a capstone imprint
capstonepub.com

This story is based on the folk tale Hansel and Gretel. It was first written down by Jacob and Wilhelm Grimm (the Brothers Grimm) in 1812, but had been told by many storytellers before. Brother and sister Hansel and Gretel are abandoned in a forest by their wicked stepmother. A bird leads them to a little house made of bread, cake, and sugar. A little old lady invites them inside. At first she pretends to be friendly, but she is really a wicked witch who wants to eat them.

The witch locks Hansel in a cage and forces Gretel to cook meals to fatten him up. At first Hansel tricks the witch into thinking he is not fat enough to eat. But the witch gets impatient and decides to cook him anyway. She asks Gretel to check that the oven is hot enough, but Gretel tricks the witch into climbing into the oven herself. The children escape…

Hansel, Gretel, and the Pudding Plot is published by Picture Window Books
A Capstone Imprint
1710 Roe Crest Drive
Nor th Mankato, Minnesota 56003
www.mycapstone.com

Text copyright © Isabel Thomas 2015
Illustrations by Mónica Carretero

Library of Congress Cataloging-in-Publication Data
Cataloging-in-publication information is on file with the Library of Congress.
ISBN 978-1-4795-8614-1 (hardback)
ISBN 978-1-4795-8752-0 (paperback)
ISBN 978-1-4795-8748-3 (paper-over-board)
ISBN 978-1-4795-8756-8 (ebook)

Editor: James Benefield
Designer: Richard Parker

Printed and bound in the United States.
009370CGS16

For Zachary Merlin Jones.

HANSEL

GRETEL

MRS. MAGGOT,
THE LUNCH LADY

HUNGRY CHILDREN

RAT

Hansel and Gretel would do anything for dessert. They spent their lunchtimes dreaming of gooey pies, giant cakes, and too much chocolate sauce.

Sadly, they had the world's worst
lunch lady. Mrs. Maggot had one rule:
NO DESSERT
for children who couldn't
clear their plates.

But she made sure her lunches were
disgusting. No one **EVER** got to taste
the treats from her dessert cart.

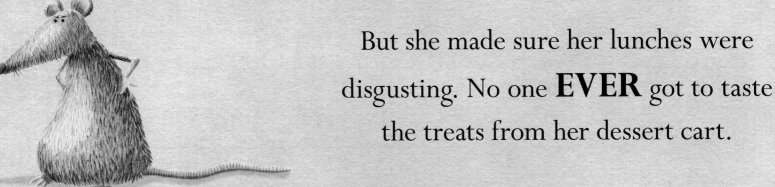

One day, Hansel and Gretel tried hiding their awful lunches. They poured pond soup into pencil cases, stashed slug sausages under the table top, and filled their pockets with pickled sprouts.

But Mrs. Maggot's nose had a knack for *sniffing* out leftovers.

"TRY THAT AGAIN, AND I'LL THROW YOU BOTH IN THE TRASH!" she snarled.

Hansel and Gretel gasped. Mrs. Maggot's last victim had reeked of rotten food for weeks.

"If only we knew where she takes that cart!" Hansel moaned.

"Don't worry," grinned Gretel. *I've got a plan.*

As soon as Mrs. Maggot's back was turned, Gretel crept toward the cart. She slipped a pencil out of her pocket and poked a tiny hole in a tub of chocolate sauce.

"Now the cart will leave a trail," Gretel winked at Hansel, "and we'll find out where Mrs. Maggot puts those desserts."

After school, Hansel and Gretel snuck into the cafeteria. They followed the trail of chocolate drops into the kitchen…

…PAST A MOUNTAIN OF MOLDY DISHES…

…AND THROUGH A CABBAGEY FOG

…to a pantry marked **"KEEP OUT!"**
So they let themselves in.

Gretel *grabbed* a mile-high lemon pie. Hansel dug into a ten-scoop ice cream sundae. They were on second helpings, when they heard a voice behind them.

Mrs. Maggot's bulky
body filled the doorway.
Hansel and Gretel were
TRAPPED.

"You've gone too far this time," growled the lunch lady. "I'M GOING TO PUT YOU BOTH IN THE TRASH."

"Please let us go!" cried Gretel. "We'll do anything!"

Mrs. Maggot **SLAMMED** the door shut and turned the key.

"OK, GREEDY GIRL!" said Mrs. Maggot. "You can wash my dirty dishes. But your brother can stay in the pantry until you've finished."

Gretel stared at the mountain of moldy dishes. It would take **HOURS**. She needed a quicker way to *free* Hansel.

Suddenly, Gretel spotted a chicken bone on the floor. She kicked it under the pantry door.

Hansel grabbed the bone, poked it into the keyhole, and *wiggled* it around.

The pantry door swung open. But it was **NOT** Gretel on the other side.

It was Mrs. Maggot, turning as purple as her pigeon pie.

"Go and open the trash bin," she barked at Gretel. "THAT BEASTLY BOY IS GOING IN!"

As Gretel climbed the steps to the stinking trash bin, one last plan *popped* into her head.

She huffed, and she puffed, and she said, "I can't lift the lid."

"Silly girl!" said Mrs. Maggot. "I could open it with my little finger. Get out of the way."

Mrs. Maggot pushed Gretel down the steps on her way up. Then she threw open the trash lid quickly.

Too quickly.

The lunch lady *wibbled,*

...she *wobbled,*

...and then she *toppled...*

headfirst into last week's leftovers.

The lid closed with a **CLICK.**

And as for Mrs. Maggot, she was taken away by the garbage collectors later that day...